# Big
# Something

## Patricia Reilly Giff

ILLUSTRATED BY **Diane Palmisciano**

ORCHARD BOOKS • NEW YORK

AN IMPRINT OF SCHOLASTIC INC.

Love to Jilli and my Jims, of course—P.R.G.

To the women of my sacred circle for their
wisdom—and for their open hearts—D.V.P.

Text copyright © 2012 by Patricia Reilly Giff
Illustrations copyright © 2012 by Diane Palmisciano

Library of Congress Cataloging-in-Publication Data
Giff, Patricia Reilly.
Fiercely and friends: the big something / by Patricia Reilly Giff ; illustrated by Diane Palmisciano. — 1st ed.      p. cm.
Summary: When Jilli and Jim see a big red structure being built next door, they imagine all kinds of frightening
things before finding out the truth.
ISBN 978-0-545-24459-6 (hardcover : alk. paper) — ISBN 978-0-545-43369-3 (lib. bdg. : alk. paper)
[1. Imagination—Fiction.] I. Palmisciano, Diane, ill. II. Title.  PZ7.G3626Fg 2012     [E]—dc23     2011016759

10 9 8 7 6 5 4 3 2 1      12 13 14 15 16
Printed in Malaysia      108
First edition, July 2012

The display type was set in P22Parrish Roman. The text was set in Garamond Premier Pro.
The art was created using oil pastels.
Book design by Chelsea C. Donaldson

# CONTENTS

## Bad News

I twirled across the lawn.
Someone was calling me.
"Jilli!"
I tried to stop.
"*Oof!*" I slid into a hole.

It was Fiercely's hole.
He was digging straight
down to China.
That dog!

"You're a mess," Jim said.
I brushed the dirt off my knees
to clean them up.
Jim leaned over.
"I have news," he said.
"Something odd is happening
next door!"

We crawled over to the hole
in the fence.
We had to see.
Fiercely stayed behind.

We sneaked past
the apple tree.
Fiercely was deep in his hole,
halfway to China.

We saw hammers
and saws and lots of tools
and men shouting.
They were building
a Big Red Something.

"Look at that weird lady," Jim said.

She wore a pointy hat.

She was laughing.

*Cackle, Cackle, Cackle.*

"I think she's a witch," I said.

"Let's get out of here."

I could just see Fiercely's skinny tail.
It poked up out of the hole to China.
"Fiercely!" I yelled.
Fiercely didn't listen.
That dog *never* listened to me.

"Run like the wind," I told Jim.
And that's what we did.
All the way to the kitchen.

# From the Window

Nana was cooking eggs.
They were a little brown
around the edges.
Jim and I liked them that way.
Fiercely did, too.

But where *was* Fiercely?
I couldn't see him anymore.
Maybe he had reached China.
I hoped he'd be home for supper.

We ran upstairs to the window for
a better look at the Big Red Something.
"It might be a prison," Jim said.
"A prison for two kids playing next door,
and a dog who is somewhere in China."

We were scared.

The woman in the witch hat

was up on a ladder.

She was painting ice-cream cones

and gumdrops on the wall.

Then I knew. . . .

"It's a Hansel and Gretel house," I said.

"She wants to eat us for supper!"

"*Yeow!*" Jim yelled.

Suddenly I saw Fiercely.
He wasn't digging a hole
to China after all.
He had dug a hole under the fence.
He was heading straight
for the witch!

Oh, no.

Poor Fiercely!

What if he never got out?

He was my best friend.

Every night he licked me
good night.

Then we'd curl up together,
in case there were lobsters
under the bed.

"We *have* to save Fiercely,"
I told Jim.
"But how?" Jim asked.

# Saving Fiercely

"We need to look scary," I said.
"Even scarier than a witch."

"This doesn't sound
like much fun," said Jim.

We dashed out to Pop's shed.
Inside it had wrenches and screwdrivers
and lots of nails.
It had a teeny gray spider
taking a walk,
and a bunch of gummy bears
stuck to the floor.

Jim found Nana's beekeeping hat.

He plunked it over his head.

It had lots of net.

It had lots of cobwebs, too.

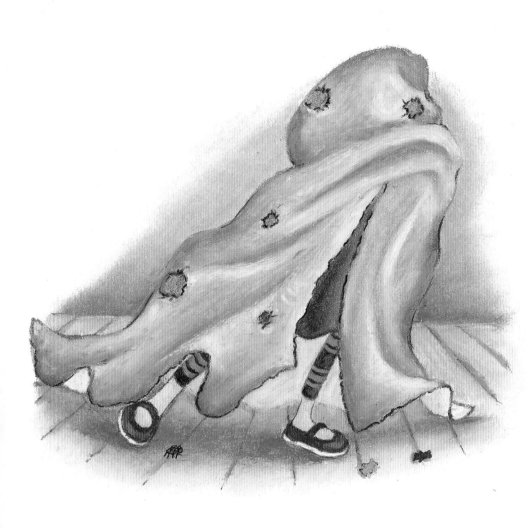

Fiercely's old blanket
was on the floor.
I hung it over my whole self.
No one could see me.
*I* couldn't even see me!

We unstuck the gummy bears
and dusted them off.
Gummy bears made you brave.
They tasted good, too.

We sneaked out of the shed.
One step. Two steps. Clunk!
I conked my head
on a big tree branch.
It was a good thing
Fiercely had chewed holes
in his blanket.
I wiggled it around.

We looked through the fence.

But what did we see?

Fiercely was on the other side.

He was chewing up the witch's weeds!

"Get out of there, Fiercely!"

I whispered loudly.

Fiercely didn't get out.
He didn't know witches were worse
than lobsters.

But I knew what to do.
I held up a gummy bear.

Fiercely saw it!

His tail flew up.

He dived back into the hole

and ran back to me!

Fiercely was saved by a gummy bear!

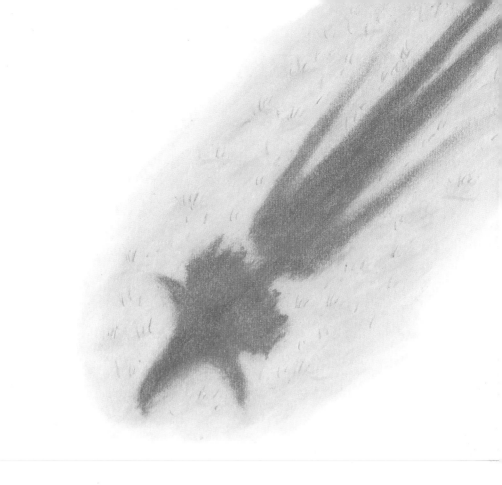

"Wait!" someone called after us.
I chomped on a gummy bear.
Jim chomped on one, too.
We had to be brave . . .
because the witch was
heading our way.

# The Big Red Something

"Grrrr!!!" I growled.

"ROAR!" shouted Jim.

Fiercely didn't say anything.
His teeth were stuck to a
gummy bear.

34

I crossed my fingers.
"I'm not afraid of witches
or Hansel and Gretel houses," I said.
"And I like the scary lobsters
that hide under my bed at night."

The lady looked over the fence.

"You're braver than I am, Jilli," she said.

I smiled.

"You're not a witch at all," I said.

"You're Ms. Berry."

Everyone knew Ms. Berry.

Nana said she was the nicest teacher.

"Soon you'll come to this *new* school,"

Ms. Berry said.

"We'll learn about real lobsters that
live in the ocean.
We'll read and make up stories
about witches and
Hansel and Gretel houses."

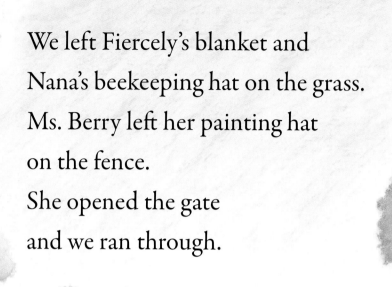

We left Fiercely's blanket and
Nana's beekeeping hat on the grass.
Ms. Berry left her painting hat
on the fence.
She opened the gate
and we ran through.

"May I help paint?" I asked.

"Me, too!" Jim said.

We had one more gummy bear left.

A red one. We gave it to Ms. Berry.

She liked gummy bears, too.

We were sure of it.

And we were sure
we'd love going to the
Big Red Schoolhouse!
*"Woof!"* Fiercely agreed!